Marvin the Strange Little Marmoset

**National Library of Canada Cataloguing
in Publication Data**

Papineau, Lucie
[Oscar le drôle de ouistiti. English]
Marvin the Strange Little Marmoset

Translation of: Oscar le drôle de ouistiti.
English Text: Sheila Fischman
ISBN 1-894363-80-9

I. Fischman, Sheila II. Sarrazin, Marisol, 1965–
III. Title.

PS8581.A6658O8513 2001   jC843'.54   C2001-900371-4
PZ7.P2114Mo 2001

Publisher: Dominique Payette
Series Editor: Lucie Papineau
Art direction and design: Primeau & Barey

Legal Deposit: 3rd Quarter 2001
Bibliothèque nationale du Québec
National Library of Canada

Dominique & Friends
Canada:
300 Arran Street, Saint-Lambert
Quebec, Canada J4R 1K5
USA:
P.O. Box 800
Champlain, New York
12919
Tel: 1 888 228-1498
Fax: 1 888 782-1481
E-mail:
dominique.friends@editionsheritage.com

Printed in Canada
10 9 8 7 6 5 4 3 2

The publisher wishes to thank The Canada Council
for the Arts for its support, as well as SODEC
and Canadian Heritage.

Government of Quebec
–Book Publication Tax Credit Program–SODEC

*For Dominique Demers,
her irrepressible laughter and dreams...*
L.P.
*For Patrick, Marie-Claude and
the entire, wonderful Léonard family*
M.S.

Marvin the Strange
Little Marmoset

Story: Lucie Papineau
Illustrations: Marisol Sarrazin
English Text: Sheila Fischman

Marvin is a strange little marmoset. Like all his brothers and his cousins and even his old grandpa, he lives high up in the foliage of giant trees.

Everyone plays and laughs like crazy as they jump from branch to branch.

All but Marvin, the strange little marmoset.

Actually Marvin has a problem; he's afraid of heights.
And if you're a little monkey, that's very inconvenient.
But what Marvin really doesn't like is when his
brothers and his cousins and even his old grandpa
make fun of him.

Marvin doesn't want to be different from the
others. Marvin doesn't like being called a strange
little marmoset, Marvin hates it when others
make fun of him.

Gilda the giraffe has called
all her friends together in her cave,
where they're sheltered from the North
Wind. "I have an idea," she tells them,
"for helping little Marvin."

And she's off! As the others look on
in amazement, she unveils a model.
"What's that?" asks Ernest the
young elephant.
"It's a big top," Gilda tells him.
"The big top for our circus."
"A circus!" exclaim
the animals in chorus.
"Yay!"

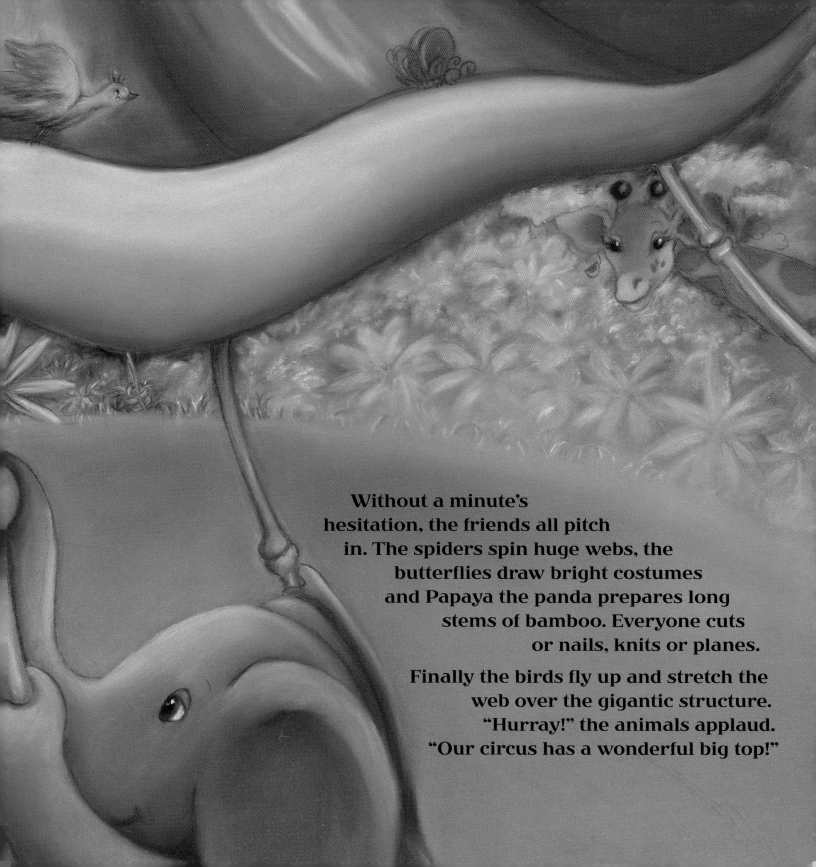

Without a minute's
hesitation, the friends all pitch
in. The spiders spin huge webs, the
butterflies draw bright costumes
and Papaya the panda prepares long
stems of bamboo. Everyone cuts
or nails, knits or planes.

Finally the birds fly up and stretch the
web over the gigantic structure.
"Hurray!" the animals applaud.
"Our circus has a wonderful big top!"

"What do we do now?"
asks Ernest the young elephant.
"Now," replies Gilda the giraffe, "we'll work on
our acts. You, Ernest, will be the mouse-tamer."
"Eeeeeek!" Ernest howls as he climbs a tree.
"I'm afraid of mice!"
The little giraffe smiles faintly.
"Exactly," she says, "exactly…"

Not far from there, on the lowest branch
of the smallest tree in the forest, Marvin the
marmoset is all by himself. And he's bored.

Kiki the koala pulls him by the arm.
"Hurry up, Marvin, we need you!"

A few minutes later, the little marmoset's eyes
sparkle when he learns that he'll be one of the stars
of the Tip Top Circus. But when Gilda tells him
he's to be a tightrope-walker, Marvin feels the
ground give way beneath his feet.

Luckily, Kiki the koala in his clown costume makes Marvin smile.
"Don't worry, little marmoset, I'll help you. Heights don't bother me!"

Kiki climbs the big ladder up and up and up, higher and higher and higher.
Then he dashes along the tightrope as if he were about to fly.
"Oh!" cries Marvin, covering his eyes with his hands.
Kiki does some funny acrobatics as he dances along the tightrope. Marvin
bursts out laughing – and the more he laughs, the less afraid he is!

Rehearsal time is over and the big
night is finally here! Backstage, Marvin's
friends are pacing back and forth.

The Ringmaster, Crumpet the crocodile,
steps into the spotlight. When the drum
rolls, he announces the first act:
Ernest the young elephant,
tamer of...

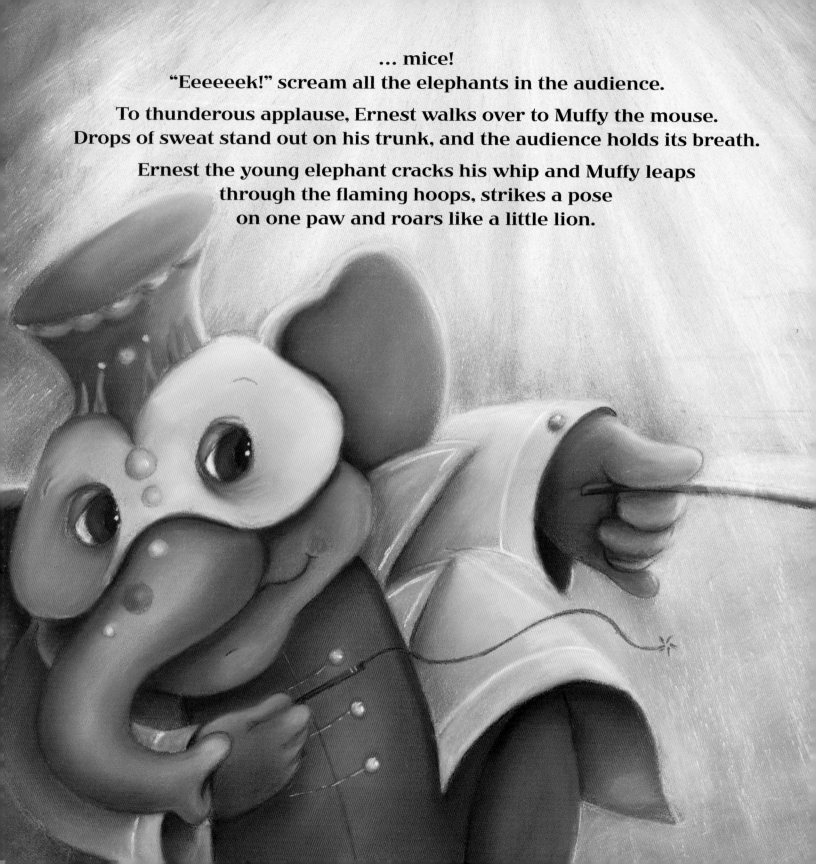

... mice!
"Eeeeeek!" scream all the elephants in the audience.

To thunderous applause, Ernest walks over to Muffy the mouse.
Drops of sweat stand out on his trunk, and the audience holds its breath.

Ernest the young elephant cracks his whip and Muffy leaps
through the flaming hoops, strikes a pose
on one paw and roars like a little lion.

"Yay! Hurray! How brave!"
exclaims the ecstatic audience.
Ernest makes his finest bow – while
standing on his mouse-tamer's chair!
All the other acts are very successful too.
The crowd goes wild when Gilda
the giraffe juggles with her spots
which have drifted away on the wind!

Marvin the marmoset has butterflies in his stomach. Kiki the koala is already pirouetting on the tightrope.
"Come up here, Marvin, you strange little marmoset," exclaims the little clown, "Come and dance with me!"

With his heart pounding, Marvin dashes into the ring. And boom! He slips on one of Gilda's spots and lands on his bum!

The whole audience bursts out laughing.

Marvin's fear is still there, deep in his stomach.
But he can feel the warm waves of laughter
gradually making it melt away...

Without looking at the ground, he climbs up and
up the big ladder, all the way to his friend Kiki
who's waiting for him at the top.
"Would you look at that," whisper Marvin's
brothers and his cousins and even his
old grandpa, "would you take a look at that!"

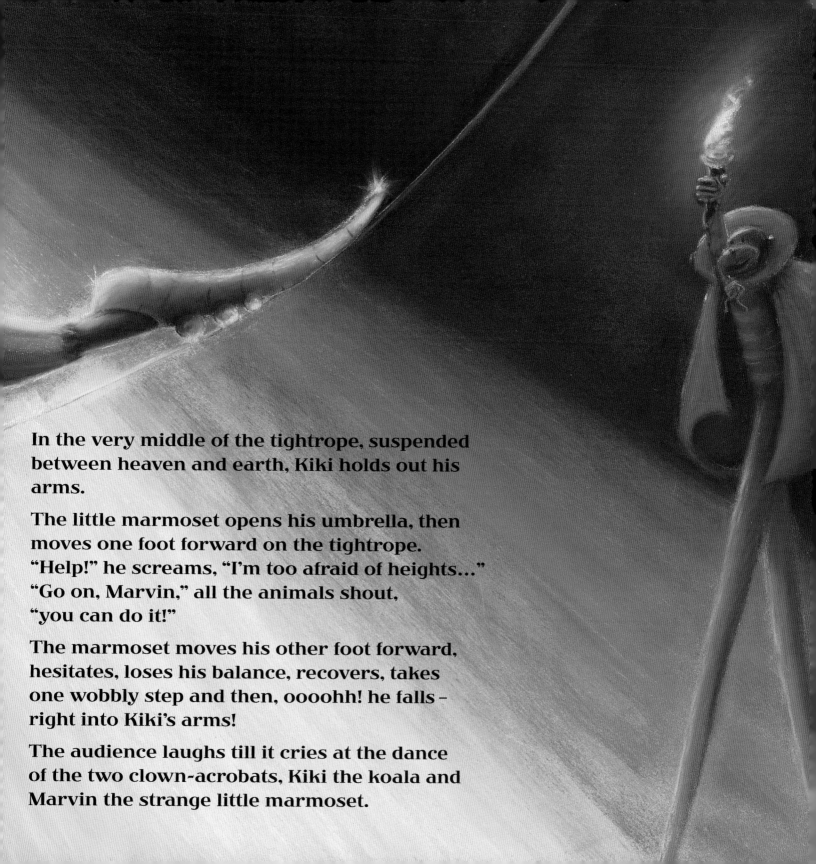

In the very middle of the tightrope, suspended between heaven and earth, Kiki holds out his arms.

The little marmoset opens his umbrella, then moves one foot forward on the tightrope. "Help!" he screams, "I'm too afraid of heights…" "Go on, Marvin," all the animals shout, "you can do it!"

The marmoset moves his other foot forward, hesitates, loses his balance, recovers, takes one wobbly step and then, oooohh! he falls – right into Kiki's arms!

The audience laughs till it cries at the dance of the two clown-acrobats, Kiki the koala and Marvin the strange little marmoset.

Now the show is over, but the party's just beginning.
All the spectators join the dance.

Marvin is smiling at the stars. Now he understands that he's
not alone. The little marmoset has the best friends in the whole
world: Gilda the giraffe, who juggles with her spots, Ernest
the young elephant, who can tame mice, and Kiki the koala,
who knows that laughter is stronger than fear.

Three cheers for the
Tip Top Circus,
three cheers for strange
little marmosets!